有一天，小紅雞走過農場庭院時看到一些穀麥。
「我可以種植這些小麥啊，」她想，「但是我會需要別人幫我。」

One day Little Red Hen was walking across the farmyard when she found some grains of wheat.
"I can plant this wheat," she thought. "But I'm going to need some help."

小紅雞向農場內其他的動物叫道：
「有誰會來幫我種植這些小麥啊？」
「我不能，」貓兒說，「我太忙了。」
「我不能，」小狗說，「我太忙了。」
「我不能，」鵝說，「我太忙了。」

Little Red Hen called out to the other animals on the farm:
"Will anyone help me plant this wheat?"
"Not I," said the cat, "I'm too busy."
"Not I," said the dog, "I'm too busy."
"Not I," said the goose, "I'm too busy."

「那麼我便自己一個去做吧，」小紅雞說，
於是她便將穀麥拿去種植了。

"Then I shall do it all by myself," said Little Red Hen.
She took the grains of wheat and planted them.

密雲下雨，太陽照曬，小麥成長起來，又強壯，又高大，更是金黃色的。
有一天，小紅雞看到小麥長得成熟了，知道現在便是收割的時候了。

The clouds rained and the sun shone. The wheat grew strong and tall and golden.
One day Little Red Hen saw that the wheat was ripe. Now it was ready to cut.

小紅雞向其他的動物叫道：
「有誰會來幫我收割小麥啊？」
「我不能，」貓兒說，「我太忙了。」
「我不能，」小狗說，「我太忙了。」
「我不能，」鵝說，「我太忙了。」

Little Red Hen called out to the other animals:
"Will anyone help me cut the wheat?"
"Not I," said the cat, "I'm too busy."
"Not I," said the dog, "I'm too busy."
"Not I," said the goose, "I'm too busy."

「那麼我便自己一個去做吧，」小紅雞說，
於是她便拿起鐮刀將所有的小麥都割下來，然後將它們扎成一捆。

"Then I shall do it all by myself," said Little Red Hen.
She took a sickle and cut down all the wheat. Then she tied it into a bundle.

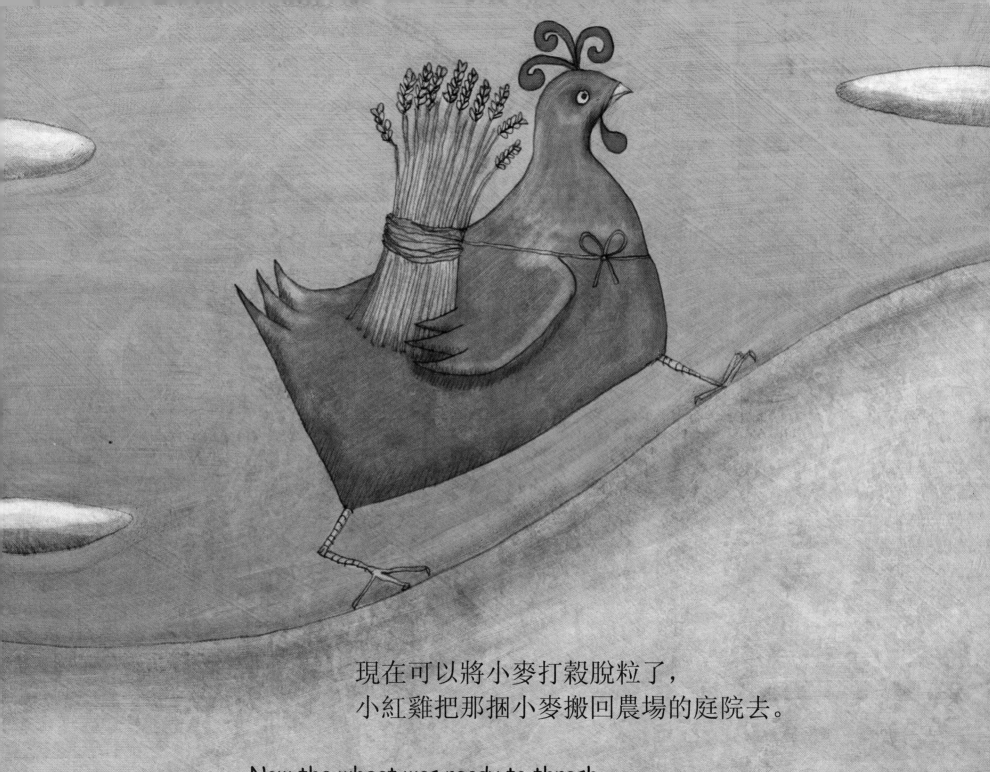

現在可以將小麥打穀脫粒了，
小紅雞把那捆小麥搬回農場的庭院去。

Now the wheat was ready to thresh.
Little Red Hen carried the bundle of wheat back to the farmyard.

小紅雞向其他的動物叫道：
「有誰會來幫我將小麥打穀脫粒啊？」
「我不能，」貓兒說，「我太忙了。」
「我不能，」小狗說，「我太忙了。」
「我不能，」鵝說，「我太忙了。」

Little Red Hen called out to the other animals:
"Will anyone help me thresh the wheat?"
"Not I," said the cat, "I'm too busy."
"Not I," said the dog, "I'm too busy."
"Not I," said the goose, "I'm too busy."

「那麼我便自己一個去做吧！」
小紅雞說，

"Then I shall do it all by myself!"
said Little Red Hen.

她花了一整天將小麥打穀脫粒，
當她做完之後，
她便把穀麥搬到她的拖拉車去。

She threshed the wheat all day long.
When she had finished she put it into her cart.

現在可以將小麥拿去磨成麵粉了，但是小紅雞覺得很疲倦，
於是她便走進穀倉，她很快便睡著了。

Now the wheat was ready to grind into flour. But Little Red Hen was very
tired so she went to the barn where she soon fell fast asleep.

第二天早上，小紅雞向其他的動物叫道：
「有誰會來幫我將小麥拿到磨坊去啊？」
「我不能，」貓兒說，「我太忙了。」
「我不能，」小狗說，「我太忙了。」
「我不能，」鵝說，「我太忙了。」

The next morning Little Red Hen called out to the other animals:
"Will anyone help me take the wheat to the mill?"
"Not I," said the cat, "I'm too busy."
"Not I," said the dog, "I'm too busy."
"Not I," said the goose, "I'm too busy."

「那麼我便自己一個去吧！」小紅雞說，
於是她便拖著她那滿載穀麥的拖拉車，一直拉到磨坊去。

"Then I shall go all by myself!" said Little Red Hen.
She pulled her cart full of wheat and wheeled it all the way to the mill.

磨坊主取過小麥，將它們輾磨成麵粉，
現在可以用它來造麵包了。

The miller took the wheat and ground it into flour.
Now it was ready to make a loaf of bread.

小紅雞向其他的動物叫道：
「有誰會來幫我將麵粉拿到麵包師傅處啊？」
「我不能，」貓兒說，「我太忙了。」
「我不能，」小狗說，「我太忙了。」
「我不能，」鵝說，「我太忙了。」

Little Red Hen called out to the other animals:
"Will anyone help me take this flour to the baker?"
"Not I," said the cat, "I'm too busy."
"Not I," said the dog, "I'm too busy."
"Not I," said the goose, "I'm too busy."

「那麼我便自己一個去吧！」小紅雞說，
於是她便把那袋麵粉一直拿到麵包店去。

"Then I shall go all by myself!" said Little Red Hen.
She took the heavy sack of flour all the way to the bakery.

麵包師傅取過麵粉，加入酵母、水、糖和鹽，
他跟著把生麵糰放入烤爐烘烤。
當麵包烤完後，他便把麵包交給小紅雞。

The baker took the flour and added some yeast, water, sugar and salt.
He put the dough in the oven and baked it.
When the bread was ready he gave it to Little Red Hen.

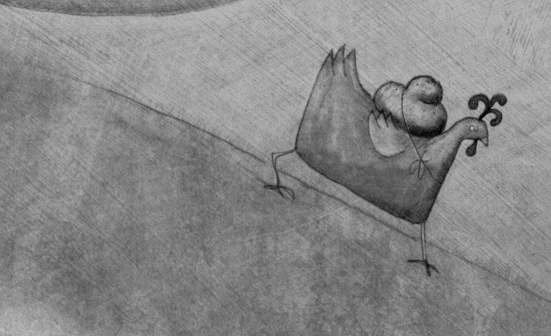

小紅雞拿著新鮮烤好的麵包一
直走回農場的庭院。

Little Red Hen carried the freshly
baked bread all the way back to
the farmyard.

小紅雞向其他的動物叫道：
「有誰會來幫我吃這個新鮮美味的麵包啊？」

Little Red Hen called out to the other animals:
"Will anyone help me eat this tasty fresh bread?"

「我會，」小狗說，「我有空啊。」

"I will," said the dog, "I'm not busy."

「我會，」鵝說，「我有空啊。」

"I will," said the goose, "I'm not busy."

「我會，」小貓說，「我有空啊。」

"I will," said the cat, "I'm not busy."

「啊！讓我先考慮一下！」小紅雞說。

"Oh, I'll have to think about that!" said Little Red Hen.

小紅雞邀請了磨坊主和麵包師傅來分享她那美味可口的麵包，而其他三隻動物只能在旁觀看。

The Little Red Hen invited the miller and the baker to share her delicious bread while the three other animals all looked on.

key words

little	小	clouds	雲
red	紅	rain	雨
hen	雞	sun	太陽
farmyard	農場庭院	ripe	成熟
farm	農場	plant	種植
goose	鵝	cut	收割
dog	狗	sickle	鐮刀
cat	貓	bundle	捆
wheat	小麥	thresh	打穀
busy	忙	grind	輾磨

flour	麵粉	tasty	美味
the mill	磨坊	fresh	新鮮
miller	磨坊主	delicious	可口
ground	輾磨	all	所有
bread	麵包	she	她
baker	麵包師傅	he	他
yeast	酵母		
water	水		
sugar	糖		
salt	鹽